"*The Summer of Dead Birds* is a near mythic journey into life-stopping loss: a howl, and a hymn to what's mortal. But in Liebegott's spare, rich language and lines (and in the silences between the lines), what is gone might blink briefly alive again—not to hold, but to love."

—**MARIE HOWE, author of** *Magdalene*

"Sweet and so sad and the writing's perfect."

—**EILEEN MYLES, author of** *Afterglow (a dog memoir)*

"A fierce, funny, agonized, cracked-open aria in homage to the presence and passing of fiercely loved things. Grippingly, heart-wrenchingly sad, it also makes me feel less alone in facing the love and loss at the core of living, which is also to say dying."

—**MAGGIE NELSON, author of** *The Argonauts*

"Brilliant! We are fortunate to have the stark genius of Ali Liebegott on earth to push our lives forward like all the best poets do."

—**CACONRAD, author of**
While Standing in Line for Death

"Full of wry heartbreak and sweet, sad humor, righteous fury and tender grief, *The Summer of Dead Birds* reconnects us with our own humanity. Ali Liebegott is never unaware of the absurdity of our lives, in all their gorgeousness and gravity, and reading her you feel on the verge of a new perspective, one that could heal all wounds, solve all mysteries, turn a sob into a guffaw."

—**MICHELLE TEA, author of** *Against Memoir*

The Summer of Dead Birds

Ali Liebegott

FEMINIST PRESS
AT THE CITY UNIVERSITY OF NEW YORK
NEW YORK CITY

Published in 2019 by the Feminist Press
at the City University of New York
The Graduate Center
365 Fifth Avenue, Suite 5406
New York, NY 10016

feministpress.org

First Feminist Press edition 2019

 This book was made possible thanks to a grant from New York State Council on the Arts with the support of Governor Andrew M. Cuomo and the New York State Legislature.

 This book is supported in part by an award from the National Endowment for the Arts.

First printing March 2019

Cover art by Ali Liebegott
Cover and text design by Suki Boynton

Library of Congress Cataloging-in-Publication Data is available for this title.

For A. J. S.
in memory of M. B. and Rorschach

The Summer of Dead Birds

Summer was like your house: you know where each thing stood. Now you must go into your heart as onto a vast plain. Now the immense loneliness begins.

—*Rainer Maria Rilke,* The Book of Pilgrimage, II, 1

Part One
Winter

I.

the birdbath is always half-empty
where we live, it can be dry in three days

this morning while I filled it
a bird the size of a dust ball tried to fly
never getting higher than an inch off the lawn

a dove sat on a nearby branch
flapping its wings slowly and sadly
the way you numbly open and close a cabinet door
when there's nothing inside to eat

finally, the dust ball gave up
fluttered inside a cinder block to hide

II.

I feel guilty leaving the birds thirsty
still, I didn't fill the birdbath
before I went out the gate to work

by the trash cans, next to my motorcycle
the dust ball faced the wall

Are you okay? I said
bending down to touch its head

immediately I thought,
I shouldn't be doing this—it's diseased

could I carry it on my motorcycle to school
and call animal rescue while I taught my class

the whole ride to work I thought,
How could I leave it?

it wouldn't survive all day huddled by the trash cans
in this neighborhood of feral cats and birds of prey

instead of teaching, I babbled to my students about the bird

You can't save everyone, the woman who raised canaries said

then later at my university job the most naive student said,
Maybe it's fine and will be gone when you get home

Do you know how sick a bird has to be to let you touch it?
I snapped

But maybe, she said

III.

after work, I rode my motorcycle up the driveway
afraid to even turn my head to where the bird had been

it had moved a few inches closer to the trash cans
I knew it had died, no bird lies down on its side

inside I postponed the inevitable, opening junk mail
then returned with a plastic bag over my hand

I picked up the tiny tea-sized sandwich
its speckled chest gray with dots, blood on its beak

the blood was actually a berry
and I knew exactly the tree it came from

every summer on my birthday you made
me angel food cake, with cream and berries

IV.

your mother was dying, it was Christmas
she sat on the flowered couch opening presents

afterward, she wrapped her bathrobe carefully around her
and stepped over wrapping paper on the way to the bedroom

she could still walk then

if you want to see time move fast
watch a fifty-five-year-old woman
go from gardening to dead in two months

your mother's death started with an aching back
after bending over, pulling weeds all day

the sore back turned out to be cancer
spread like stars across her body, into her spine

she told me she had cancer before she told you
she wanted me next to you when she called

when she did, you paced around the back deck listening

I tried to stay close to you as you paced
holding our pet bird in my hands
pressing my nose into its feathery neck

V.

our bird turned into my bird when we broke up

I never wanted that bird, you said
an impulse pet-shop buy after a hard family visit

I wanted to name the bird Nabokov
but you didn't want to *commemorate a pedophile*
the only name we could agree on was Angel

I'd been afraid of Angel dying since day one
but that means nothing since I'm afraid
of everything dying all the time

the first thing I do when I come in the door
is check that the pets are alive

after we broke up, Angel suddenly died

just a few weeks before, I told myself
I was going to stop mourning things that weren't dead yet
then I walked in the house and there was no peep

cup full of husk, her tiny body on the bottom of the cage

I put her body in a tea box and carried her to the sea

that was after I froze her, cried hysterically,
and asked my therapist if I should have an autopsy done

at the beach, I stood on the rocks
and tossed her body into the breaking waves

she looked especially tiny in the ocean

I had expected her to sink or get swept away
but she became stuck in a tide pool
swirling between the rocks

the sun had set, it was almost dark
I left her spinning there

VI.

it was winter break and overcast
you listened to your mother tell you she had cancer

I followed at a respectful distance, Angel cupped in my hand

I don't know how she escaped to fly onto the neighbor's roof

we didn't have a ladder so I piled rickety chairs
on top of each other until they were high enough
I could reach over the fence

Angel sat huddled, a stunned pile of blue feathers

I climbed the tower of chairs, broom in hand
trying to nudge her toward me, inch at a time
terrified I'd scare her into flight

when she hopped within arm's reach
I grabbed her, relieved

I came down with my hands cupped around her
an imaginary bubble to keep her safe if I fell

your mother's surgery was scheduled
as soon as you hung up the phone
you went inside to pack

VII.

after your mom's surgery I drove up to join you
my tire blew two hours from Fresno

I stood on the side of the highway
while the sun went down and called AAA

behind me a train track forged its way through a field of weeds

I don't know where the thought came from:
This is the kind of place where people are abducted by aliens

I grabbed a metal pipe from the bushes and clenched it
waiting to protect myself from errant light beams

we didn't know your mom would be dead
less than two months from this night

her own body abducted cell at a time

VIII.

I waited two hours for the AAA guy

he couldn't find the dyke on the side of the road
warding off aliens with a metal pipe

when he finally arrived, it took another hour
to pry the rusted spare off the bottom of my truck

at your mother's house you sat next to her bed watching
    the Food Network

you hated that she only wanted to watch cooking shows
while she was dying and could barely eat

I kissed her forehead when I walked in

that was when she could still talk and drink without a straw

each day she could do so much less
it's so much less each day for a person to die in two months

she wanted to talk about the awfulness of the flat tire
the injustice of waiting so long for AAA

I was embarrassed she would waste any part
of her evaporating life discussing the flat tire

so I pulled up a chair to watch the cooking show, too

IX.

your mom's friends called her BB
it stood for blackbird

does a bird say goodbye before flying off
a tiny peck at shared seed, a feather pluck
nothing?

you'd been estranged from your mother for years

still at the end you came running
fluffing her pillows, straightening the bedsheets

X.

your mother's mantel was crowded
with your artwork and photographs of you

looking at it, you didn't seem estranged

but I'd known all the birthdays and graduations when
    she didn't come

XI.

as she grew worse, I entered the dark bedroom
in the back of the house less and less

I busied myself with laundry, dishes, groceries,
and caring for the dogs and cats

I carried a bucket around the backyard
scooping up moldy dog shit

sometimes you'd come outside to smoke

when you did, I'd set the bucket down and hug you
these moments we were alone together were rare

XII.

it's terrifying to go into a room where someone's dying
even if you've been in those rooms before

to push open the bedroom door
and find the right thing to say to the vanishing body

only the dying person knows the right thing to say

I'm thirsty, or when the pain's so deep, pure gibberish
the drugs do the talking after the hallucinations start

you slept on a cot next to your mother's hospital bed
so you could get up every two hours and dole
out her pills until she could no longer swallow

then you carefully lined up syringes to feed into her IV
a tray full of syringes, all different doses

I sat on the couch with friends who'd already lost parents
and knew how to go through taxes and receipts
and sort out your mother's life

on one of the last days she could speak
when no one was pretending she wouldn't die

she said she wished she was well enough
to take one last drive and see the cherry trees blossoming

her bedroom was the chamber where the two of you healed
and I guarded the gate, shooing the dogs away

so they didn't do what they desperately wanted
to jump on your mother's bed and lick her delicate face

XIII.

the laundry was made up solely of your mother's pajamas

the drawstrings became tangled around the agitator
I struggled to free them but they wouldn't budge

this was the first time I cried, it didn't matter if I freed them

your mother wasn't going to live long enough to wear
    them again

XIV.

the dying need groceries, too
and you bought your mother the best of everything

the most expensive juice and pudding
the softest pajamas and highest thread count sheets

the last thing you fixed her was a milkshake

she woke up thirsty in the middle of the night
and whispered, *You're going to kill me*
because she knew you were exhausted

you were giddy at her hunger
after days of eating nothing

she drank the whole thing down,
burped, and asked for another

your tired hands made another milkshake
she drank that one, too

and then you crawled onto the cot and slept next to her
your tired hands next to your mother's tired hands

XV.

the refrigerator had become a coffin
of things your mother could no longer eat
a spectrum of solids to liquids

I asked if I should throw out the pudding
since it had been so long since she'd eaten it

you weren't ready
the milkshake had given you hope

you wanted the pudding to be there
in case she woke in the night and asked for it by name

XVI.

a hospice worker was sent to the house
in the final days to examine your mother's feet

she said they were mottled

the word rolled around my mouth like a marble

mottled, when the bottoms of the feet
get spotted because the blood isn't circulating

we asked the nurse many questions
but really we were only asking one

Do you know when she'll die?

the nurse said, *It's important to not cling to the dying
often they hang on if they feel the living holding on*

but who could not hold on to their mother

XVII.

it was late morning, the day she died
I know exactly how the sun beat into the back of the house

you came into the hallway and called me
Will you come sit with me and my mom?

she couldn't talk anymore but she could listen

you told her we were there and loved her
and she should go if she was ready

we saw her hear you

Just keep walking, don't be afraid
I'll go with you as far as I can, Mom

I couldn't imagine being brave enough
to shove my mother's raft on its way

but she started to go, we felt it

Don't look back, we'll be taken care of
just keep going, Mom

and she did

XVIII.

She's still warm, you said, touching her forehead

how did you know to close her eyelids

we sat with her for a while
then went in the yard to smoke on the steps

a few feet away on the other side of the French doors
her body still lay in the hospital bed

the whole time she was dying you had to sneak cigarettes
because the smell made her sick
all her senses heightened after chemo

a fire truck went by and you howled like a dog

that's what your mom did when she heard sirens
she howled to prompt her dogs' howling

XIX.

you lit candles while Valerie stood behind
your mother's body and sang "Amazing Grace"

you removed the IVs from her arms and placed them
on the tray where her next round of medications waited

I held her stiffening body as you rocked it side to side
trying to free her arm from a pajama sleeve

twice you tried to pull the catheter
from between her legs, but it wouldn't budge

XX.

I learned from you how to prepare a body

you filled a bowl with soapy water
dropped in perfume and rose petals

dipped the washcloth in the rose water and moved it over her
cleaning around the stubborn catheter last

then you dried her gingerly with a towel
and spread lotion over her arms and each finger

we looked at her closet of shoes

everyone but me knew not to leave jewelry on
because it would be stolen at the mortuary

when she was completely prepared
you put your fingertips on her forehead and kissed her

you waited hours before calling the hospice nurse
to tell her your mother had died

because once they sent someone for her body
it would be taken away forever

XXI.

for hours we were high from your mother's death

I know it's hard to imagine the word *beautiful* here
but we were there and know it's the only word

the grace that filled you as you held her hand and told her
to keep going, to not be afraid, to not look back

when you finally called the hospice worker
she said they'd send someone to come pick up
the hospital bed and medications and walker

we'd forgotten about the walker
it seemed like an eternity since your mother had walked

XXII.

we waited for the paramedics in the driveway
smoking and making phone calls

retelling the story of her beautiful death
to everyone in her phone book

the ambulance surprised us
it pulled up without sirens on

two polite men slid a gurney out the back
unsnapping each of its wheeled legs

I was afraid of seeing your mother's body taken away

they gave you a moment alone to say goodbye
and then zipped her inside a bright-blue body bag

and pushed her on a gurney out the dim hallways of
    her own house

XXIII.

your mom wanted her ashes scattered in a stream
that held water she was baptized with late in life

the stream was on top of a mountain
accessible only in summer, located by a handmade map

I watched as you listened, eyebrows raised
hovering over her bed as she whispered this request in her
     final days

but you promised her everything, even though
you had no idea how you'd get up that mountain

Part Two

Crying Season

I.

you took the pillow that propped her head up
plump, like a pillow in a coloring book
big down marshmallow with a goose-head tag

and walked around the house
trying to pull the scent from its depths
at night you wrapped your arms around it and slept

I'd never been around grief this big, it scared me

long after her scent was gone
you kept the pillow propped on your bed

II.

Few lesbian relationships survive the death of a mother,
my therapist said

I was so mad when she said that
We will, we will, I thought

III.

after I left you I had nowhere to live
so I moved into my tiny writing studio

the only place for my bed was behind a window
a few feet from a noisy bus stop

while I lay awake waiting for daylight
my thumb searched my ring finger in the dark
looking for the missing silver band

it hunted helplessly, like a dog that runs up
to every person on the street that resembles its dead owner

IV.

first thing in the morning
my dog Rorschach and I walked to the coffee shop
when we returned, I opened the blinds and sat down
    on the bed

the people at the bus stop ate candy and drank sodas
letting their wrappers drift away behind them

sometimes they watched me inside my diorama

did I say diorama, I meant aquarium

and I was the fish that swam in small predictable circles
waiting for Crying Season to begin

V.

have you ever been lost like this, hours spent facedown
unable to understand how you ended up
with your heavy limbs or the tattoos that cover them

at night, Rorschach settles her old dog body
next to mine with no regard for my grief

during the day, I sift dumbly through milk crates
filled with eight years of cards and presents

there are two pictures of us at the amusement park
on our first date after you admitted cheating

each of us alone on a green bench, our young faces
smile cautiously from behind the same stuffed pig

VI.

and then the walking began

I set out with Rorschach and made giant loops
of the neighborhood from morning until night
trying to know how to live next

we walk past the car wash where the stalls are full at six a.m.
who washes their car at six in the morning?

Rorschach loves my grief
it means she gets to walk twelve hours a day

at night when I return to my studio and take off my shoes
my toes have bled and scabbed to my socks

VII.

while Rorschach sniffs the foot of a tree
I try to understand the therapist's suggestion:

Ask yourself what you need every half hour
and see if you can give yourself that

I need to call the dentist to fix the teeth I've shattered
    in my sleep
I need to see if the flattened pigeon's still in the gutter

I found it the first night I moved out of our house
and now I check on it daily like an old neighbor with
    a bad hip

I understand how a bird could get hit by a car, but flattened

in its blissful pecking at a cigarette butt, it never felt
the dump truck reverse over its skull

two days ago, the sweeper flipped the flattened pigeon
from the gutter to the middle of the street

the tips of its wings fluttered like newspaper edges
each time a car ran over it

VIII.

this land of flattened pigeons in Pompeii poses
wings upraised and trying to flap away from their bodies

two puffed-out pigeons seduce each other by dancing
and pecking the ground dangerously close to their
    flattened brother

I pray they won't begin to eat him
(urban pigeon myths depict such things)

I'm begging you not to do what you're thinking,
I say to the young lovers

if my therapist were here I'd say,
I desperately need the in-love pigeons not to eat the flattened one

IX.

who will help me sweep up the puff of dust and plaster
that tumbles down inside me after each depression

every hammer swing sends pieces of drywall, scuttling
down my chest to settle in my hollow legs

I've become a walking urn of my own ashes

it doesn't matter, worthy or unworthy depression
the ashes gather at the same winter rate

X.

Rorschach will be thirteen in a few weeks

I want to ask every stranger in the street,
What's the oldest dog you ever knew?

it's early and bright, the street apocalyptic in its emptiness
like a Sunday, but it's not

Rorschach tugs to get a good sniff of the flattened pigeon

It's real, I want to say
not a photographer's pawn
dressed up in tatters, face streaked with soot

no makeup man lifting up those wings
pretending the edges of a last-minute escape

but no one needs to tell Rorschach what's real

XI.

when she was two, I got Rorschach's name tattooed
    on my back

I accidentally insulted the tattoo artist
by double-checking it was spelled right

he wanted me to know he'd been tattooing for twenty years
I was less worried about him than the dyslexia of
    consonants in her name

it was my second tattoo ever and when the needle dug
    into my back
I felt a rush of electricity travel up my spine

XII.

do you know how a goodbye can make you curious?
suddenly there's a million possible streets to explore

Rorschach leads me down a street draped in electrical wires
I follow, lost in thought, listening to the electricity popping
    above me

my thoughts are:
Do goodbyes happen years before the actual goodbye?

my thoughts are:
Can leopards change their spots if you wait long enough for the leopard?

XIII.

I follow the crackling wires as far as they'll lead me
it's true I thought, if the wires fall and these pops turn
    to sparks

we could lie down and feel them on our faces like rain drops

Rorschach was walking more directly under the wires
she would be the one to get it if they fell

did I mention I was trying walking meditation?

XIV.

the first time I meditated I saw a man
push the point of an ice pick into my sternum

next, in a Mexican restaurant at a friend's Quaker wedding

I spent the first twenty minutes staring at a vent
wondering if a sniper was crouched in there

and if so, should I break the silence to warn the other guests

during the second twenty minutes, I worried I had Crohn's
    disease

XV.

Rorschach tugs toward the gutter
she wants to piss on the flattened pigeon

after a divorce, does everyone float like a lost balloon?
their head, a forest of rotting animals

we walk past the tire shop and I worry
about how I'll cope when Rorschach's gone

every couple blocks I lean over and smell her head

I used to say, *When Rorschach goes, I go*
but now I'm older

I'm older and she's older

XVI.

to live with a dog is to have it become part of your body

the first time I was separated from Rorschach
I dropped her at a friend's house the night before a flight

when I returned home to pack
the absence of her sounds was profound

no nails clicking across the floor
no tail thumping into a doorframe

even though she was only a year
I already knew which sounds would go when she was gone

to live with a dog is to grow old with a dog

this is how you lean over to help your blind dog down
    the steps
this is how you lift your arthritic dog onto the bed

this is how you greet the deaf dog after work

look for her in every room until you find her asleep
then stand panicked in front of her until her chest moves

XVII.

my life changed the day I brought Rorschach home
three months old and tiny spotted legs

I put a blanket on the floor a few feet from my bed
she'd stay for a second then scuttle over to me
with her tiny puppy legs

each time I carried her back, I gave a half-hearted *stay*
immediately she returned to me

after five times I gave up

in the middle of the night I woke
to her suckling the bottom of my T-shirt

the whole reason we were doing this dance
was because everyone said,

Don't let the dog sleep in the bed with you
you'll never be able to discipline the dog after that

but the whole point of having a dog
is to let it sleep in the bed

XVIII.

I'd stop looking for dead things
if there'd stop being dead things everywhere

the last day of Crying Season it poured
Rorschach refused to go out in the rain

I walked through the park to the coffee shop
a black spot in the green grass caught my eye

a dead blackbird

I thought about moving or burying it
something besides leaving it unceremoniously there

then I saw another and another

big and small, their heads tilted to the side
ants crawled over their feathered crowns and eyes

the sheen of black feathers became undeniable through
    the blades of grass

here it was, the summer of dead birds

XIX.

it's impossible to not think *apocalypse*
when the ground is covered in dead birds

there were so many I wondered if I should
take one to prove they were real

a few blocks up I waited at a stoplight
next to a boy on a skateboard

I wanted to ask him to follow me
and show him the dead birds

but the light changed and he skated off

it felt creepy to ask and anyway
some kids can shrug their shoulders and say,
Oh well, the park's filled with dead birds

but I was never that kind of kid

XX.

lately, Rorschach's back legs give out midtrot
a quick scrape of nails on sidewalk

C'mon old lady, pick those back legs up
fear in my voice as I say it

after weeks of walking in circles around the neighborhood
it's come to me we're training

the weight of my grief equal to the food we'll stuff in
    our packs

say farewell to the flattened pigeon
put your paw on my thigh while I drive

I'll blow the cigarette smoke away from your face
come, despite that it's summer and your back legs are weak

we'll go all the way to the cliff edge
I promise to stay close, my hands on your hips to steady you

let's go to a cave big enough to dump this sorrow

Part Three

The Summer of Dead Birds

I.

it's the end of May and the sky is filled
with birds being little whores

dipping and weaving across the freeway
following each other recklessly
out of the bushes and into oncoming traffic

this is the kind of courtship I understand
one lover throwing themself in front of a car
every four seconds in order to seduce the other

every time a bird nearly misses my windshield, I gasp

after the fourth bird I give up worrying,
light a cigarette, and propose a toast

Here's to being little whores, I say

II.

once a bird dipped right into the path of a burgundy sedan
an explosion of gray feathers

a few minutes later the driver pulled onto the shoulder
and sat stunned behind the wheel while his hazards blinked

I think of that bird a lot
and the stunned driver

thank god, I've never hit an animal

my uncle has totaled car after car
running over a plethora of deer

it's so dark on those country roads
and the deer come out of nowhere

III.

remember when we were little whores
weeks into our love affair on women's land?

I was hallucinating because I'd abruptly quit drinking
you were taking hooker baths in the tent

in between, we were fucking like nobody's business

the month I met you I was starting a new life
trying to put something down
without picking something else up

as much as possible I pretended
there weren't objects floating around me

I crawled around a field with my sketchbook
trying to capture the poses of a hundred dying bees

I thought they were tame, friendly even
because they didn't fly away when I came near

later I found out bees tiptoe delicately around right before
    they die

I drew portrait after portrait of their hairy legs and
    thick yellow sweaters

this was in the beginning when we still wanted to give
    each other everything

IV.

we both love dying things more than we let on
and we let on quite a bit

if it's true we're dead, I won't know how to love this
every wreckage, the beginning of something else

Look at us beginning, says the tiny pulsating water bubble
Hi, nice to meet you, I'm the loam that grew a heart

V.

when I figured out you were cheating on me
I told my therapist, *Thank god I'm not a violent person*

she looked at me astounded
my body full of self-inflicted wounds

I was a dumb dog, drugged and waking from anesthesia
walking into walls, half-dead, trying to wag

the deep-orange bile came years later
I didn't even know it was inside me when I heaved it onto
    the rug

VI.

I'd been shooting at the wrong target for months

you were in your bedroom across the hall
talking to your trick or writing her letters

our apartment was big and cheap
we both had a bedroom to hide in

in mine, I began a portrait of myself
pushing an oil pastel hard into the closet mirror
outlining my sunken eyes and worried brow

I kept correcting my eyes, making them sadder and sadder
then I gave myself a stick body and got a hammer

VII.

I wanted to swing the hammer harder
than I've ever swung anything

for the head to go through my head drawn on the
    mirrored door

but I was afraid to make too much noise and wake
    the neighbors

really I was afraid to lose my shit

I tapped the hammer lightly onto my face and the mirror
    shattered

it broke because it was cheap, not because I broke it

VIII.

it was maybe midnight
when my impotent shatter made you knock

What's going on? you said
I'd been asking the same question for months

I opened the door slightly as if you were a solicitor
the heavy hammer hid behind my back
pulling on the tendons in my shoulder

I could see you were worried
until now I'd swallowed every bit of fear and left you
    out of it

but now part of my blue pastel eyelids lay on the floor
    at my feet

IX.

nobody's perfect
I did my share of lying, too

it's impossible to know in the lying moment
which lies we'll be unable to recover from

X.

things do just disappear all the time
people and dogs and children

your mother went fast
then us

poof
my bags were packed

no way to know whose shoddy limbs
will crumble off the torso first

XI.

imagining Rorschach gone is like imagining the earth gone
I know each is slowly going but to imagine it

the scientists have shown us graphs of the hole-filled sky
disappearing bees and birds plucked from oil slicks

there are new kinds of scientists now like ER surgeons
sent to coax polar bears off broken ice floats
and take pictures of islands made of plastic bags

we're running out of room for our trash
but we're still here with our skin intact

the barge of garbage far enough away
enough of the bees' work already done

XII.

The dog will start closing up shop, my coworker said
They stop eating and drinking and wagging

I do things on purpose to make Rorschach wag
now that she's almost blind with an arthritic spine

every day I bribe her to keep the shop open

I greet her dramatically with wide arms
stop at each hamburger stand

carry her up the stairs she's fallen down

she's a foot behind, stiff legged in the crosswalk
an old dog stopping traffic

I walk backward in front of her
trying to coax her all the way across

XIII.

I'm typing this with my hand on Rorschach's thigh
she's running in her dream

the irony is she's so old she can barely walk
I watch her legs move in sequence

tiny flips of her calloused paws
a quiver of her pink, spotted lips as she barks

everything is spotted on a Dalmatian
not just the fur

the roof of the mouth, the inside of the lips and ears

XIV.

you think a dog is old until it gets even older
her gaunt back hips, the lumpy body getting lumpier

Rorschach sleeps on the bed with me
coughing through the night
her throat a road in winter, impossible to clear

I follow her around with a tissue to wipe her running nose

before she jumps off the bed
she pauses afraid not able to see

I say, *Come on, Rorschach, you can do it*
or I lift her with my bad back

XV.

Rorschach's sweater is amazing
a gray-and-lavender argyle turtleneck

she looks like a scholar
without it she shivers

the other night when I took it off to wash it
her hips looked so thin

XVI.

Rorschach's senile now
sometimes when I hug her she tries to bite me

she sleeps all day with her fading hips
her old dog lip curled back

I put my hand under her belly or leg or paw
the heat of her dog body against me

when she's gone I can only imagine it
as the sadness of wanting a tangible god

Part Four

The Official Center of the World

I.

in a few days it will be Rorschach's thirteenth birthday
today she had pre-birthday pizza and pre-birthday French fries

it's her new habit to press her paw into my thigh while I drive
my new habit is to touch her ears as much as possible

I don't ever want to forget how they feel

I push my nose into the fur at the top of her collar
try and memorize her smell

I do it again and again until she growls at me

it's difficult to smell her neck, dodge being bit,
and the whole time not crash the car

would it be fucked up
to get Rorschach's ears taxidermied after she dies?

what do people normally do with their dead pets' ears?
I want to have something to hold
during moments of great despair when she's gone

during moments of great despair now
I hold her until she tries to bite me

and then in a few hours I try again

her taxidermied ears could be like handkerchiefs

if I promised not to wring them would it still be fucked up?

II.

what if you leave knowing there's nothing where you're going?

but you go anyway, you need the *going*
the hand out the window, the red rocks, all that

the hot wind blowing in the window, the back of your T-shirt
stuck to the seat, wet with sweat

you need to find a humble beaten god
like a bad petting-zoo goat
always shooed for gnawing the wall

a god like a bar buddy
with a flawed and sloppy past
knuckles fucked from punching walls

finding this god is dire, the same way it's dire
to sit next to the right person in the breakroom
after a friend's suicide

a god who'd never say anything stupid
who'd understand how a person could climb
the bleachers of a football stadium and jump

how this complex sorrow, holds inside it
the possibility of all our climbing legs

III.

people say anything to the ones they love

they say, *I'd give you my kidney*
I'd bury you with my own hands
I'd do anything, god forbid, that day comes

in the last days of your mom's life
we begged you to let us take care of her for a few hours
while you got a massage

you'd been by her side nonstop for months
your back knotted from leaning over her hospital bed

you agreed, but only if I promised to keep her company
while you were gone, to talk to her, she could still hear
even though she was no longer talking

terrified, I examined her face while she slept
her eyelids closed heavily from the drugs
I was thankful every time she took a breath

I forced myself to take her hand
I'll take good care of your daughter, I said

when I said it she grunted so loudly it scared me
I couldn't tell if it was gratitude, a threat, or a plea

it shook me but when you came home
I didn't tell you about her grunting or my promises

I don't know why

did she know I'd only be able to keep my promise for a year?

IV.

out the car window
are snapshots from my marriage

my marriage
drowned, resuscitated, drowned

the final fall, haphazard
a slip on the sidewalk, a cracked skull

then we were facedown and drowning
in the tiniest puddle of our own blood

I'm spreading my fingers as wide as I can to let the air
    rush through
Rorschach's hips are warm from the sun coming in

she's sleeping a deep, old-dog sleep
lip curled back on the seat

a bump in the road wakes her and she opens her eyes

V.

everything wasn't always heavy

once I called you from a pay phone
and asked you what you were doing

in your sweetest voice you told me
you were feeding honey to a dying bee

it could hardly walk, tiptoeing slowly
along the edge of the saucer

after an hour, it had the strength to fly away

VI.

I want to choose the cancers in my book
the breakups, the deaths, and the impending deaths

it's summer and Rorschach's wearing a fur coat
I'm taking her on a road trip for her birthday

I promise this is the last trip, I say to her panting head

it's clear I'm the only one looking for an earlier self

VII.

I hate the idea of not knowing your dog is sick

you think the dog has pulled a muscle
and that's why it's suddenly limping

or you think the dog is just a little sleepy

dogs can't mumble in bed in their sweaty pajamas
next to a nightstand covered in half-eaten puddings

I hate that dogs can't say a slow, measured goodbye

VIII.

Felicity, California: The Official Center of the World
Population: 3

I wish there were trees but we're in the desert
just trains and rocks and occasional signposts

this is what I wanted, right?
hundreds of miles to pull my dead marriage from me

and leave it fluttering in the road behind

The Center of the World is currently closed
and open by appointment only

Please call for an appointment to visit the Center of the World
or the Center of the World Gift Shop

if the gift shop had been open I would've bought a postcard

postcards and birdcalls are the only things I ever buy in
    gift shops

IX.

thirteen years later I'm still trying
to figure out the things Rorschach notices

we pass a car dealership and she looks back
at a long string of balloons

You want balloons, I'll buy you balloons, I want to say

I follow out the window the things Rorschach's watching
until I've almost driven off the road

the sound of my tires crossing the ridged shoulder
startles me and I swerve back on the highway

Rorschach's weak back legs can't hold her up
and she slams into the windshield

I'm so sorry, I say
which is quickly becoming our mantra for the trip

X.

the car dealerships and fast-food joints disappear
deeper into the red desert

everything's red and white for miles

I drive next to a red-and-white rickety school bus
filled with farm laborers

a bright-white water cooler tied to its bumper

the bus tows two outhouses that bounce up and down
kicking up cyclones of red dust

Rorschach's head follows the spinning dust like a
    dipping bird

XI.

I've been loading an imaginary gun
in my head for hundreds of miles

I'm pushing a bullet into the chamber

that same action repeats itself in my brain
as often as every thirty seconds, I started timing it to see

why does my brain keep doing that?
I was just petting Rorschach's ears or lighting a cigarette

the image pops up like the terror of forgetting an
    appointment

sometimes I'm wiping my pants
and the way my thumb moves to get the chocolate off

is the same pressure I imagine I'd use to push a bullet into
    the chamber

it's a black revolver, the bullets are gold

I've loaded many guns but never a revolver
mostly I've loaded double-barrel shotguns

you slide two bright-red plastic shells into the barrel
the red plastic looks like the torsos of toy men

my father used to sit in the garage with thousands of
     empty shells
he had a machine that held gunpowder and buckshot

when he pulled the handle, the torsos folded up neatly
     on top
like tiny origami envelopes

there should be a trophy for people who still show up
     for work
even though the whole day they're competing with images
of their own enormous hand, sliding gold bullets into
     a revolver

XII.

I never understood people who said the desert was beautiful
but now I see they're right

when the sun is going down
and all the cactuses stand tall and independent

I purposely didn't use the word *cacti*

the fact that *cactuses* isn't a word
is definitely an indication of what's wrong with this world

XIII.

it's late when I try and pinpoint
when we began our drift from one another

remember when we drove across the desert
at night with no air-conditioning?

the only station that came in was wing-nut talk radio
water had just been found on Mars
and all the kooks were calling in

Call in, you said, *call in*
miraculously I got put on the air

the best question I could come up with was
Were there ducks paddling around that water on Mars?

the wing nut talked excitedly in circles never answering
    my question

but we laughed so hard, a late-night exhaustion cackle
that lasted long enough to get us home

XIV.

I want the emotions of coloring books
each feeling to remain perfectly contained
inside its own thick black line

grief, utterly grief
joy never seeping into anger

here I am, not forgetting you at all
like a dog I drag our corpse from room to room

in the bedroom where your mother died
a tiny bit of Fresno light always seemed
to sneak through a fold of curtain

how does a person dislodge the scenes
that burn inside them like arsoned cars?

XV.

I've never seen cremains but I've been told sometimes
finger-sized bone lies among the ash

it's these pieces that upset families
who want to sprinkle their loved ones like fairy dust

not have them plunk, heavy, like nickels into the sea

the cremains of our marriage shift grotesquely inside me
good and bad memories mixed in different-sized pieces

sometimes when I can't sleep I think
irrationally, with my whole body

You're almost forty now, you can't be smoking
even if I've smoked myself that day

in my absence, I still want to protect you

XVI.

the best thing about the desert is there's almost always a train
    going by
shipping freight cars stacked like colored blocks to the base
    of the sky

I wish the gap between those boxcars was my birthplace
I understand the risk of losing legs to hop a train

and that horn, who doesn't want to fuck to that sad shit?

I drove for a long time beside a boxcar with doors open
    on both sides
a moving window

I stared through the window to the rest of the far-off desert
I wanted to stick my enormous hand through that gap
and touch the other side

to throw the revolver through, then the fistful of bullets
the gold bullets would scatter like sparks

like the beauty of driving behind a tow truck at night
    dragging nothing
the chain hanging off the bumper, all those sparks
    flying up

I could hide my most treasured things on the other side of
 that moving window
my most treasured things aren't mine yet

Rorschach's taxidermied ears, neatly wrapped in paper

XVII.

on the motel bed I do leg lifts hoping to recuperate
despite my failed knee surgery

it's when I'm falling asleep that I feel you gone completely
like someone's removed a bone from my leg
and the flesh has collapsed around its absence

XIII.

a few days after we broke up, I went to an old friend's house
the only thing I could do was weed her tomato garden

I pulled and pulled until the back of my neck was
    bright red

she lived near a train track
the horn kept wrapping itself around the bay

after we were done she put the sprinkler on
and went inside to cook dinner

I stayed outside
a hummingbird came and sat on the wire tomato cage

at first it flew over to the water hovering in the air
dipping its long beak into the stream, then coming
    back out

XIX.

Become nothing,
my friend says every time I start to cry

I don't understand
Don't become the thing that tries to overthrow the grief

she draws me a map to the suspension bridge
a few-mile walk to the scenic view
the whole time I walk, I try to become nothing

the wind pushes hard into my face as I cross the bridge

boats with boarded-up windows fill the bay
a new pier is built next to the old one

a broken boardwalk bows gracefully into the sea
the planks lead right into the bottom of the water

XX.

towns can get abandoned just like children
the town built next to the prison shut down
now there's no one left to buy a hamburger

everything is exhausted

the cactuses and the closed-up gas station
hover in the dark in their deception

weeds grow at the feet of the gas pumps
trash bags caught in cactus patches and barbed wire

what goes up must come down

down with the prison that took all the money to build
push the lever, let it fall

XXI.

in our beginning, we were writers from San Francisco
driving through the Blue Ridge Mountains
lost and speeding, late to our show in a rickety van

still, we pulled off the road to roll down a hill into a meadow
all twelve of us lying at the bottom giddy and dizzy

you came toward me out of the laughter
one hand behind your back holding a bunch of wild flowers

I'd seen you pick them and more than anything
hoped they were for me

XXII.

I hate that everything dies, marriages and dogs and mothers
each death its own snapshot, sweaty in my hand

it's astonishing how long the body can remember grief
I turn over in the night and there it is

pushing hard against my rib cage like a doorframe
stretching its agitated shoulders

a galaxy of grief swirls inside me
I've become the cavern I want to visit

each loss begins as a single drop of water
struggling to roll off the ivory edge of a rib

until it begins to harden
and hangs, a stalactite tomb

XXIII.

on a dirt road that runs beside the paved one
an ambulance winds through the mountain to
    the power plant

no services forty miles

a Border Patrol truck hidden behind a bend
waiting in case someone manages to survive
crawling through the desert in hundred-degree heat

in Texas every mile I pass a sign that says *drive friendly*
an important reminder in a state that allows drivers
to carry firearms and open containers of alcohol

for twenty miles I get stuck behind a truck trailing
    a prefab home
I stare at the back door of the house imagining sullen
    teenagers smoking on the steps

the problem with burying things is
even if it takes millions of years
the buried thing always finds a way to emerge

XXIV.

what if I don't even know the beginnings of forgiveness

it's elusive like a word on a billboard in a foreign country

the same word next to a picture of a flat tire,
a gear, or two crudely painted ovens

I guess at *repair*

I could repair a tire or an oven or a gear

right now, the only words I understand are

the dust, the barrel of nothing

XXV.

it's Rorschach's birthday
we wear birthday hats and I sing to her

in the motel room we eat pizza and watch TV

someone told me Dalmatians are the only dogs that smile

Rorschach was born with a jet-black patch over her eye
as she got older the white hairs slowly overtook the patch

now the patch is almost white
the tide line moving farther up the shore

tomorrow we'll start our journey home
wherever home is now

Rorschach walks in a few small circles on the bed
then finally settles down, her body alongside me

I close my eyes and concentrate on her head resting
    on my leg
I want to remember the exact weight of it

Acknowledgments

I've been blessed with an exceptional, loving writing community my entire career. Many friendships and fellow writers have sustained me during the writing of this book. Thank you to all of them. In addition, thank you to the San Francisco Foundation and the RADAR Lab for supporting early drafts of this manuscript.

Thanks to the following people who directly helped me during this book's many incarnations: Justin Chin, CAConrad, Marie Howe, Kevin Killian, Robin Coste Lewis, Eileen Myles, Maggie Nelson, Ariana Reines, sam sax, Michelle Tea, Karolina Waclawiak, and Matthew Zapruder.

Justin Chin, rest in peace. You are so missed.

Deep thanks to my agent, Kristyn Keene at ICM.

Thank you, Lauren Rosemary Hook, and everyone at the Feminist Press for your thoughtful support and hard work on this manuscript.

A second thanks to Michelle Tea, for championing all my books into print. I am forever indebted to you for over twenty-five years of literary friendship.

Lastly, to my better half, Beth Pickens, I love you so much. I'm sorry you have to live with an insane writer. Thank you for supporting ALL my artistic endeavors.

The Feminist Press is a nonprofit educational organization founded to amplify feminist voices. FP publishes classic and new writing from around the world, creates cutting-edge programs, and elevates silenced and marginalized voices in order to support personal transformation and social justice for all people.

See our complete list of books at
feministpress.org